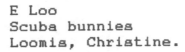

For Kelly G., with whom I first went diving —C. L.

For Tomer and Amit —O. E.

Text copyright © 2004 by Christine Loomis. Illustrations copyright © 2004 by Ora Eitan.
All rights reserved. This book, or parts thereof, may not be reproduced in any form without permission
in writing from the publisher, G. P. Putnam's Sons, a division of Penguin Young Readers Group,
345 Hudson Street, New York, NY 10014. G. P. Putnam's Sons, Reg. U.S. Pat. & Tm. Off.
The scanning, uploading and distribution of this book via the Internet or via any other means without
the permission of the publisher is illegal and punishable by law. Please purchase only authorized
electronic editions, and do not participate in or encourage electronic piracy of copyrighted materials.
Your support of the author's rights is appreciated.
Published simultaneously in Canada. Manufactured in China by South China Printing Co. Ltd.
Designed by Gunta Alexander. Text set in Friz Quadrata.
The art was created using mixed media, including computer techniques.

Library of Congress Cataloging-in-Publication Data
Loomis, Christine.   Scuba bunnies / Christine Loomis ; pictures by Ora Eitan.
p.   cm.   Summary: Scuba-diving rabbits have adventures which include swimming by a pirate ship
and encountering a variety of sea animals. [1. Scuba diving—Fiction. 2. Rabbits—Fiction.
3. Marine animals—Fiction. 4. Stories in rhyme.] I. Eitan, Ora, 1940- ill. II. Title.
PZ8.3.L8619Sc 2004   [E]—dc21   2002153866   ISBN 0-399-23465-9
1 3 5 7 9 10 8 6 4 2
First Impression

Scuba Bunnies

Christine Loomis

Pictures by Ora Eitan

G. P. Putnam's Sons ✏ New York

Scuba bunnies
Long to see
What's beneath
The deep blue sea

Kiss their mamas

Check their gear . . .

Tanks are filled

Masks are clear

Watches working

Wet suits zipped

Snorkels on

Flippers flipped

Scuba bunnies

Bold and brave

Sink beneath

A rolling wave

Poke and peek
In secret places

Peering into

Fishy faces

Floating, drifting

In the blue

Bunny buddies

Two by two

Bunnies dive
Bunnies dip
To a sunken
Pirate ship

Sharks are circling
Hungry, slow
No treasure here
It's time to go

In a rush
Of rising bubbles
Buddies swim
Away from troubles

Scuba bunnies
Safe and sound
Friendly dolphins
Gather 'round

Across the waves upon the tide
Bunnies on a dolphin ride

Past otter papas with their pups

Octopus with suction cups

Whales who sing so sweet, so low
Of moonlit seas
Of long ago

Past tortoises
With great green shells
Buoys clanging
Mournful bells

Back again
The dolphins fly
New friends wave
A sad good-bye

Scuba bunnies

In a row

Do the backstroke

Home they go

Mamas welcome
    Bunnies back . . .

Hug them, dry them
    Fix a snack

Hold them curled up
In their laps
Scuba bunnies
Take their naps

Waves come whispering from the deep
Bunnies answer in their sleep

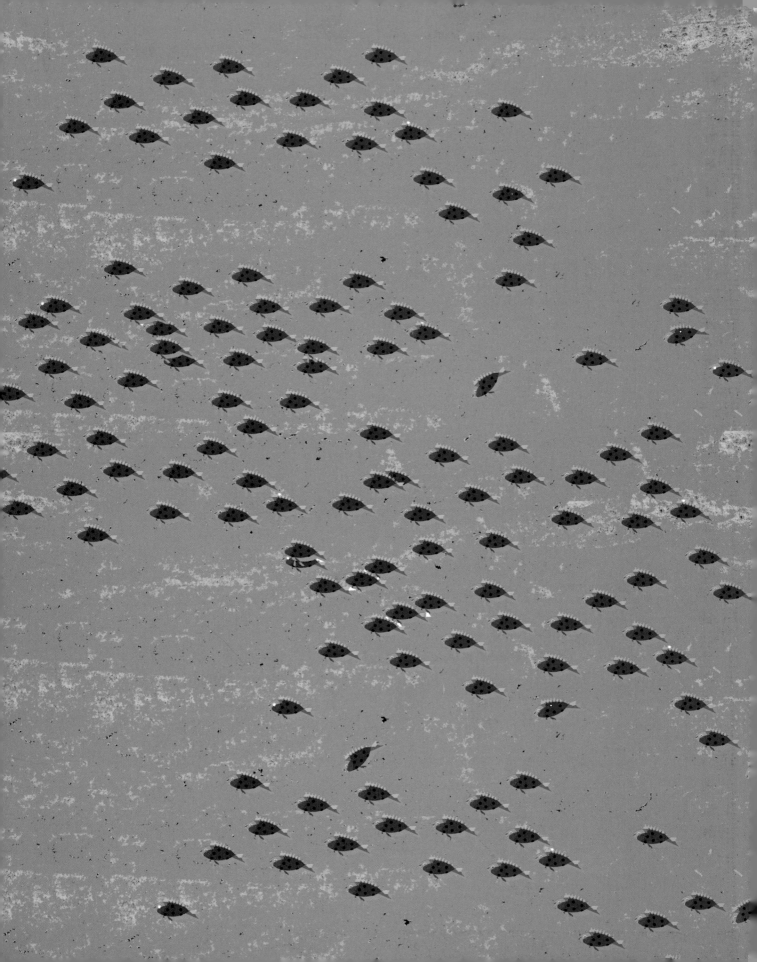